Grady Miller

A Very Grady
Christmas

GRADY MILLER BOOKS

COVER PHOTO by Don Goodman
(**ship2me@gmail.com**)

COVER DESIGN by Yevgen Kaminsky
(**yevgenkaminsky@gmail.com**)

Please contact the publisher at:
gradymillerbooks@gmail.com

1236 1/8 N. Cahuenga Blvd.
Hollywood, CA 90038

Contents

Christmas in Los Angeles

He had a crystalline gaze that resembled a junkie's, only the brightness came from a natural source. Lawrence Brown was newly converted to the Christian faith.

He was a camel-faced, chocolate-colored man who worked to the wee hours at the airport, unloading travelers' luggage from the cars and taxis that paused in front of the terminal. He looked handsome and respectable when he went to work in the shirt he ironed himself and the narrow necktie of his navyblue uniform. The squalid room, lowly job, and simple food that he prepared himself supplied him with enthusiasm. He took them as sacraments in his new life, for Lawrence was awakening from the vapors of drug addiction.

On a table below a radiant portrait of Jesus, Lawrence feverishly wrote letters to his wife who was in Sybil Brand. This pretty-sounding name belonged to the women's prison of the county of Los Angeles.

In Sybil Brand, Lawrence's wife had found God, too. On the reverse side of the envelopes that arrived every three days, she drew crucifixes and scribbled messages: "Christ Savior," "Jesus Loves You," and their names, Joy and Lawrence, watched over by a childishly drawn Christ.

Lawrence Brown was the first person I rented a room to, so he was sort of special. At this time I managed a rooming house in one of the dicier parts of Los Angeles, taking care of a decrepit two-story house at the corner of Estrella Ave. and 22nd Street that had happily sheltered a Victorian family. Now, its peaked roof sheltered a small version of the United States, with all races represented: all, I say, save one.

But a good representative was nearby, the Korean who owned the little grocery cater-corner. His store boasted a half-finished painted image of the Virgen, indeed only the crudest outlines made by some negligent muralists who had left Guadalupe's face blank and forgotten to color in her robes. But there could be no mistake: it was the Virgin. Miraculously the image had survived gang-bangers' bullets and buckshot that pocked the outer walls of the corner store.

"Oh the gunshots and the graffiti," the Korean moaned, "they keep me awake at night!"

The bags under his eyes deepened, and his skin

tended to a sickly yellowish tone. He soothed his nerves listening to classical music in his store. All in all, he seemed poorly prepared for the ersatz war zone we lived in.

A young couple from the same town in Mexico, Pedro and Taba, shared the lower floor of the house with me and Lawrence Brown. Before, our rooms had been, respectively, the dining room, a washroom, and a parlor. Pedro and Taba worked in a sweatshop on one of the top floors of a downtown building, amid the ghostly glow of fluorescent lights and the clamor of sewing machines. Another couple lived with them, Adán and Delfina, also from the south of Jalisco, and we all chatted amiably in the kitchen, and they helped me out with my Spanish.

The electrician who lived on the floor above had already reviewed Taba's body lustily with his bloodshot eyes, and his asides left no doubt about what he would do if he were alone fifteen minutes with the young woman.

Like myself, Mack was employed by the owner of the house. He was blond and mustachioed, in his early thirties, with a ruddy face that betrayed his uncommon fondness for beer. Every morning, when he left to work at one of the owner's twelve houses, two cans of Budweiser hung from his leather tool belt. Mack and I were the gringos of the house.

When Christmas season came, Pedro and Taba

proposed having a gift exchange and, what's more, having a Mexican-style barbecue. It was their first year in the United States, and a barbecue, or *barbacoa*, would help ease the aching nostalgia they felt for their homeland.

I gave my permission, but there remained the problem of Mack. I preferred that he knew nothing about the barbecue. Mack, hothead that he was, would object because, after all, we were going to dig a pit and have a bonfire practically in downtown Los Angeles. Mack would scream bloody murder, and he'd call the fire department, or something like that.

Christmas Eve came. Pedro and Taba and the other couple went to one of the cities neighboring Los Angeles. Thanks to the culinary tastes of the local Mexican population, there was a butcher shop where it was possible to select and slaughter a goat. Afterward, they cut some broad maguey leaves from the garden of a house in the Sunset district.

Christmas day the sun shone through the milky veils of smog, this sad and hopeful sun that bathes the days of Los Angeles. Around noon, the neighbors loaned me a shovel and we began to dig a pit over three feet deep. Pedro and Adán placed mesquite firewood and lit it. When the wood was turning to embers, they put a layer of bricks on top. Then we took the boxes of butchered goat out of the fridge and, wrapped in cloth tarp, the hunks of meat were placed over the hot bricks, folding the broad maguey leaves on top, with more bricks above, and everything covered once again with shovelfuls of earth. All day long the meat cooked slowly in the mesquite embers.

The house filled with rich smells of punch that simmered on the stove. Aromas of cinnamon, guava and sugar cane thrilled our nostrils. Later the punch was served hot with a shot of tequila.

Mack leaned on his elbows out the second floor window and toasted us with his can of beer, each time more raucously. I was surprised that he hadn't made a single complaint about the *barbacoa*.

"It smells gooood!" Mack shouted when he came downstairs to get a beer out of the fridge, and then returned to his room, where hard rock pounded. In the living room we sat and drank soda and punch with much expectation. It was the best part of this fiesta, waiting while the goat slowly cooked deep in the earth.

Night came. Taba and Delfina prepared salsas in a stone molcajete, and they heated tortillas on the stove. We put wrapped presents in a corner of the sitting room. Mack came back down for another beer and, opening it, he said, "I'm so hungry, I could eat two horses."

He returned to his room and the speed metal blasting out of his stereo. Soon we heard from upstairs the sound of the doors slamming and the shouts of Mack and another tenant, then more doors slamming. Those of us in the sitting room exchanged looks and I thought, "Now Mack is going to spoil everything with a fight."

We were just about to sit down to the feast of goat's

meat, when I heard a very loud knock on the front door. I went to answer. There stood two uniformed from the L.A.P.D.

"Does Mack Murphy live here?" they said languidly as two cops working a Christmas Eve. "We received a call about a disturbance."

They came up the stairs. First door on the right, I pointed out. Into the hall came another tenant in a purple satin robe, David, a timid office worker with Afro hair who had been shouting.

David spent more time than a girl in dressing, combing and perfuming himself, and now he had a voice more hysterical than any girl's, explaining that he had complained about the loud music to Mack, and Mack had punched him in the arm.

"Open the door. Police," they said to Mack's closed door. "We want to talk to you."

After a few moments, Mack's brick-red face appeared in the crack, and they asked him if he had struck David. He denied it. David shrieked that he was a liar, and lifted up his satin sleeve to show the bruises on his scrawny arm.

"It's not necessary, sir," one of the cops told him. Meanwhile, the other cop looked over Mack's shoulder: the walls of his room were decorated with street signs, from the Santa Monica freeway, the famous intersection of Hollywood and Vine, and a stopsign.

"Those your signs?" they asked him. "You know, sir, that having these is in violation of the law."

Mack insisted that he had found them in the closet

when he moved into this house—they'd belonged to a previous tenant. Despite his vehement protests, the cops took him away and he spent Christmas in jail. Poor Mack. I would've liked to have seen him there, among thieves, murderers, rapists, and drug dealers, trying to explain how they arrested him for having some lousy street signs.

In the end, we had our feast of goat's meat, white and tender, with its slightly smoky flavor that melts on the tongue. In the sitting room there piled up dirty plates with goat bones picked clean, empty bottles of beer and cans of soda. For a long time there was only the contented sound of chewing and drinking and the tinkling of glasses being replenished. Afterward, we were stranded on the living room chairs, stuffed full of food and toasts.

Long past midnight Lawrence Brown arrived from the airport, and we invited him to have some goat tacos. The camel-faced man wanted none of it. He withdrew from us with a withering look as if we were lepers, a look that said, "Thou art sinners. I will not feast on the meat of horned beasts and gulp liquors like thyselves, and dull the senses, cloud my mind, and sully the temple of the body. I can already imagine all of you sizzling in the flames of hell, shouting for God's mercy for having strayed from the good path."

He turned his back on us and shut himself in his room to stick to the narrow path of righteousness and write a letter to his dear Joy, who was spending Christmas in the women's jail.

The next day Mack called from his jail to wish us a merry Christmas and tell us he regretted having taken the signs from the streets of Los Angeles.

For Santa

Miracle on Cahuenga

Two weeks before Christmas my six-year-old daughter wrote a letter to Santa Claus, addressed to the North Pole. In the letter she asked for a doll, a make-up kit, and a limousine. Yes, a limousine.

As an extra sweetener she enclosed two crisp dollar bills. She then sealed the envelope, addressed it to the North Pole, and badgered me to get a stamp on it. After reminding me every five minutes to take it to the post office, I finally obliged her and scribbled our return address on the envelope before dropping it into a mailbox on Fairfax.

Christmas came and New Year's, desultory with the impending end of celebrations, sped by on its heels. Then the rat race, temporarily halted by the holiday season, launched anew. It was already the second

Wednesday night of the New Year and I brought Galaxia home from the baby sitter. I opened the gate to our house and saw the outline of a bundle in the dark. My immediate thought, *Who put this garbage in my yard?*

I lifted it, noting its heft, and a scent of fresh vinyl drifted to my nose. In the darkness, I made out a tag, "To Galaxia. . ." How many people knew we were living here in this exact location? Only a handful. We'd just moved to Cahuenga Boulevard a couple of months ago. And the giver managed to get the belated bundle to our improbable address, which includes 1/8. Then in the dim light of the living room, I read the rest of the tag: "Your $2 is inside the make-up kit. Santa."

The bag, decorated with angels, contained a ballerina Barbie, a change of doll clothes and the pièce-d'-résistance, a make-up kit, hot pink vinyl fringed by glossy patent-black trim, dotted by white polka dots and a mini-Eiffel Tower motif. Lift up the flap, and the case, lined by hot pink velvet, contained a dazzling array of paints, powders and enough cosmetic paraphernalia for a troupe of budding divas. It was crowded with a powder puff, a mirror, a satin sleeping mask. Four kinds of glitter powder, three kinds of lip-gloss, four bottles of nail polish, and body glitter. In the first drawer, fitted with a tiny silver handle, eye shadow all the colors of desert paintbrush; the second drawer contained hair bands with stars and pink and purple daisies, a comb and fake fingernails that Galaxia wanted to put on with Super Glue. And yes, folded inside the kit were the two dollars, the same crisp two dollar bills she had enclosed in the letter to Santa Claus.

My daughter was still poring over her new goodies as I found a note inked in felt tip in a round, clear, readable script:

Dearest Galaxia,

I hope you like your presents this year! I can see you smiling right now. Make sure you work very hard at school and love and respect your friends and family!

Love, Santa

I, who had sent the letter to the North Pole with jaundiced adult expectations, was flooded with the magic of it all. Since this mysterious delivery happened, the glow has never left and I want to share it with the world. There *is* somebody wonderful out there, doing magical things and leaving a legacy of cherished moments. On the other hand, my daughter wasn't so impressed by Santa or the inexplicable appearance of the gift; she couldn't wait to show off her super duper new cosmetic case to her school friends. But at six years old she was still unjaded and innocent enough to overlook the fact that Santa forgot the limo.

Now my daughter is older, and some of us who gathered around the Christmas tree the year of Santa's late visit won't be around this year's tree. My daughter is quickly becoming young woman. Maybe she will forget to write Santa Claus this year, I don't know.

Here's what I can tell you from our encounter with Santa: he doesn't seem to waste time on wrapping paper and ribbons. He may run a little behind schedule, so stop fretting about late Christmas cards or last minute shopping. He wants us to have everything we dream of. So dream as much as you can and tell someone about it. And know that there is real magic in the world. Go out and create it.

A Christmas Card

"How was your weekend, dude?" Ace would ask by the coffee machine. Inevitably. Bernie dreaded the question, ensnared in the feeling that he was always two laps behind in the rat race. Ace was always doing manly stuff, riding a Harley, getting a new tattoo, playing paintball, jetting to Chicago.

When Ace tortured him with How Was Your Weekend, Bernie was petrified no TV or music was handy to blot out the persistent inner voice that taunted him: *You don't have a life.* It was awful, yet once more the desire for coffee that Monday morning won over Bernie's aversion to seeing Ace and enduring the question, "Hey, dude, how was your weekend?"

After an awkward pause, in which he dribbled coffee on his freshly laundered white shirt, Bernie managed to reply:

"I was gonna send out my Christmas cards, but somehow didn't get around to doing it. One thing and another. "

"It's only October, Bernie," Ace said. "Isn't that early for Christmas cards?"

"Well, you can be sure they arrive. You can't trust the postal service. And with the holiday rush, you can never be too careful, you know."

"Nobody even sends cards, any more," said Ace. "It's all Internet."

By now Bernie was ineptly dabbing the coffee stains with a wet napkin and not even looking at Ace.

"How 'bout you. How was your weekend?"

"I went skydiving," Ace said. "What a rush."

"Skydiving?" Bernie said. He'd heard perfectly well, but distrusted his ears. "How could you do it?" Bernie said, "I could never do that. Me, a wimpy CPA."

Awed, Bernie inspected his co-worker for physical signs of change, a firmer jaw or hairs suddenly white at the roots. The change was subtler—Bernie detected a new radiance and quiet confidence in Ace. At a singles bar that evening Bernie did something highly unusual for him: he lied. He told a divorcee, overweight with beautiful eyes, that he had gone skydiving.

"You must be very brave," she said. "I could never do something like that."

She was impressed. Bernie was impressed that she was impressed: he saw the effect the lie had on her. Or maybe it was the vodka. Soon she and Bernie were smooching in the parking lot—his lie about skydiving brought him this far—and he was moving his pale, pudgy fingers surely down her back and toward her waist. Skydiving must be an aphrodisiac, Bernie thought.

They were kissing and he was pawing her hips. The divorcee took a break from kissing and asked if he went down in a tandem jump. Bernie gaped at her like somebody who's forgotten English. "I saw on TV where they don't let people parachute alone anymore," she said. "They freak out."

His hands froze.

"Did you really go?" She pulled herself from him and straightened her slinky blouse. "You're lying to me, aren't you? I could never have a relationship with somebody who lied to me the first time we met."

This got under Bernie's skin: he may have lied but he was not a liar. A week later he was compelled to climb inside a tiny aluminum bird and banzai out the side hatch at 14,000 feet, no more protection than his regular cold-weather weekend clothes, an old knitted sweater with holes in the elbows and jeans. Either that or Bernie must face up to being the pathetic loser that he was.

During the first flight into the ozone, he trembled and prayed. Eight other first-time jumpers huddled in the aircraft. He was to go third. Bernie wondered how this contraption stayed in the air and kept a hand welded to the cabin wall at all times as if the plane depended on him to stay aloft. Deathly afraid Ace would needle him about not having the guts to jump,

Bernie could only think about what would happen if his parachute didn't open. He'd drop like an egg that had rolled off the edge of a table. Since it was his first time, Bernie would jump in tandem with a trainer, but he was prey to dreadful images of a trainer having an aneurism and rendered unconscious. This reminded him of the first time off the high dive, tilting over the chlorined water, blue as a sapphire. "Don't look down," the P.E. instructor, Coach Belcher, bellowed. Wooziness gripped Bernie's stomach, he clutched it, recoiled into his snail shell and shimmied down the high-dive ladder, its metal rungs like cleats in the soles of his feet. *Loser, coward, loser, coward.* . . .

Now the wind in his face, grinding propellers in his ears—no turning back. When the hatch opened, the freezing air fogged his goggles. When the mist cleared finally, Bernie and his trainer were all alone; everyone had already jumped. Except Bernie.

The trainer clipped his harness to Bernie's and launched him into cold, open space. Eyes shut, he plummeted into blue oblivion. Opened his eyes, and was blown away by the sweep and beauty and carving wind. Bernie couldn't breathe, the air whistled by, hard and cold as tombstone marble. He had to suck hard through his mouth, forcing a slender stream of air into his lungs. As Bernie was plummeting the skin on his face rippled. Then he emerged into a space of perfect stillness when it felt as if he were floating. Then the senses came ablaze: he was an eagle, a rock, a dandelion, a blue jay, a kite, was nothing, an atom of air.

Bernie dizzied hoveringly over the patchwork of earth, cavorting between cotton-candy wisps of clouds he wanted to scoop up in his hands. At 6000 feet the trainer gave the signal to pull the ripcord. Enthralled by it all, Bernie was oblivious.

So absorbed was Bernie Callahan, hanging suspended over the patchwork of the earth, lush greens and parched browns, an intense speck, that felt boundless, he forgot about the ripcord. Forgot to yank the cord as the earth zoomed from a speck to engulf him in a dirt mattress. Bernie Callahan forgot, too, that the trainer, harnessed to his hip, had his back. Till the last fraction of a second, the sudden remembrance of the ripcord was enough to whiplash him to cardiac arrest. Soon there whooshed open a silk lotus that scooped up the atmosphere and put the brakes on his free-fall. His feet touched grassland, his heels skidded to a halt. The jump was exhilarating as hell. In a bar later, Bernie cracked jokes, a flush glowed in his cheeks. He bought a round for the other jumpers. "You da man," said Ace, who'd come to join him, and they high fived.

"I almost forget to pull the cord," Bernie cried and clutched his chest in mock horror.

"You still da man," Ace told him. "Even if you forgot the cord and your trainer had passed out, the 'chute triggers automatically at 5000 feet."

"I'm ready to do it again," Bernie exclaimed, turning away from the bar. "Right now."

He sprinted toward the door. It took the strength of Ace and two other jumpers to drag him back into the bar.

After that first jump, the sky was always tugging at Bernie. The endless columns of numbers he daily worked with lost their charm. Poof! Their magic of drawing him into to their alluring perfection where every penny is accounted for and everything balances or it doesn't: it was a realm of holy certitude. So seductive because it was something he could do perfectly. It was either right or it wasn't, no two ways about it. Bernie was good at what he did. The deep satisfaction accounting afforded was his security blanket and served to hold life's messiness at bay. Now that he faced fear head on, and leaped out the side of a plane, the security blanket was torn to shreds. Accounting, he realized, hadn't been his life, but a living death.

He was two people now—the CPA and the daredevil. The next three weekends, after an intense round of training, Bernie jumped solo. The distinction between down and up vanished: there was only *is*: borderless, unbounded being that transcended his old skin, now losing its fluorescent tan and acquiring a ruddy glow. There was no down.

The girls at the office noticed a change. He walked with a new swagger; he started swearing freely and smiled more often, unashamed of his crooked smile. One of the secretaries stopped and said, "Whoah! I never heard you cuss before. You always said dang instead of damn, and shoot instead of—"

"Wow, it just kind of came out of me."

His mother was worried sick. "You're going to kill yourself," she despaired. "You're gonna plunge like an egg off the edge of a table and splat on the ground like a rotten tomato."

Mrs. Callahan made a vile expression at the imagined gore. Bernie tried to explain, with the certitude he usually reserved for obscure crannies of tax law: "The parachute triggers automatically at 5000 feet of altitude. It's OK."

"Bernie, you're gambling with your life," she said.

"You're right," he said. "Before doing this I didn't have a life *to* gamble."

"Look, if you give me a heart attack over this skydiving, you'll live with the guilt."

In the past, he would have heeded his mother's words and curtailed his risky new activity. Now was different. He jumped whenever he could, each time more at ease. When he and Ace met by the coffee machine Monday morning they couldn't wait to share their newest adventures. On the fifth jump, right before Christmas, Bernie was master of the whole bleeping universe.

Gazing at the clouds and the birds floating past. Seeing little ant cars on the ground and ant people creeping along. Feeling the wind rake across his body. Keeping his cool when the parachute cord jammed; he knew that at 5000 feet the automatic trigger would kick in. Mr. Placid, that was Bernie. Panic never coiled its freezing fingers around his neck, nor coaxed a lame *Oops!* out of his windpipe, and his total belief prevailed as the automatic cord played coy for a split-second. In that split second Bernie Callahan slipped from here to infinity.

At Bernie's funeral, Ace endured the gauntlet of meeting his parents, nieces and aunts and uncles—on top of facing yellow heaps of potato salad at the post-memorial dinner. Ace, who'd first sung to him the praises of skydiving, was devastated by what happened to his friend. His parachute failed—a one in a million freak.

Ace started taking apart events with tweezers. He wallowed in the torments of "If only." If only he'd had a flat tire and been late for work, then he would never have seen Bernie at the coffee machine and infected the milquetoast accountant with the skydiving bug. If only Ace had found it in his heart that pivotal Monday morning to give something to the panhandler outside the office. That panhandler was a talker who might have detained him and delayed his rendezvous with Bernie. Today he might have been free of the crippling weight of his death.

Now Ace shuddered, remembering how Bernie's mother looked at him the day of the funeral, a look that said, "You murdered my son."

After the funeral, Ace succumbed to an orgy of atonement: stayed home, drank cheap wine alone, and went without shaving. He stopped going to movies and clubs, the spark of his personality faltered and dimmed. He stopped making people laugh in the market checkout line, stopped flirting with women in his apartment house laundry room. He wept like a baby whenever he replayed his friend's his last phone message—a maudlin new pastime often indulged as chaser to a bottle of wine:

"It's the weekend before Christmas," Bernie intoned in fuzzy fidelity. "I'm so psyched for the jump. It's my gift to myself."

In a kind way—there were no angry words or raised voices: it was all very hushed and discreet—Ace was quietly told that his services were no longer required at the company. His supervisor palmed the company car keys and concluded brightly: "Hey,'bro, you'll have plenty of free time to skydive."

The supervisor saw Ace flinch and apologized, "That was very insensitive me."

Another holiday season came, and along with the tinkling of Salvation Army bells, it now brought the ache of Bernie's death. On Christmas morning Ace trudged up fourteen flights of stairs to the top of an office tower. The door to the roof was wide open and he approached the edge. Looking down at the traffic in the midday glare fourteen floors below, the abyss whispered sweet nothings in his ear: "Come to me," it said, "Come," and all his sky jumps eased the way for this moment. Ace longed to feel the wind ripple across his face again. He looked over the edge at the creeping traffic below and pictured himself sprawled on the top of a taxi, another victim of something Isaac Newton had discovered long ago.

Ace was still a convict of this planet as the new year began. The unemployment checks were being replaced by eviction notices in the mail when there arrived a lost sojourner, a final straggler to the party. The worn, smudged envelope came long after the presents had been opened and the bright wrapping paper consigned to the garbage, a letter rejected by his old address, well-traveled and ricocheted between zip codes at last to his new address, a final Season's Greetings. Inside the card Bernie had scribbled:

Thanks to you, Ace, the anticipation of the next jump and the sweet memory of these weeks have been a foretaste of heaven. I am alive, yes, fully alive, for the first time in God knows; alive—my heart—rusty indentured servant clotted by disillusionment and envy—soars and swells with the eagle. My heart gets bigger like ripples from a pebble in a pond, taking in the wind, the stars, then the mountains and every blessed thing. I am invincible. Nothing can touch me—not even the kiss of earth, hammering my eyeballs out of my head and shattering me into a zillion pieces. Invincible. I have at last realized what you always knew, Ace, life isn't something you have, it's something you give. Living is giving.

Bernie's promise of absolution, from beyond the grave, restored Ace to life.

Photo by Don Goodman

ABOUT THE AUTHOR

Grady Miller grew up in the heart of Steinbeck Country on the Central California coast. More Bombeck than Steinbeck, Grady Miller has been compared to T.C. Boyle, Joel Stein, and Voltaire. He briefly attended Columbia University in New York and came to Los Angeles to study filmmaking, but discovered literature instead, in T.C. Boyle's fiction writing workshop at USC. In addition to *A Very Grady Christmas*, he has written the humorous diet book, *Lighten Up Now: The Grady Diet,* the popular humor collection, *Late Bloomer,* and the thriller, *The Hostages of Veracruz.* His humor column, *Miller Time,* appears weekly in The Canyon News (**www.canyon-news.com**)